Poppleton
IN SUMMER

Read more
Poppleton
books!

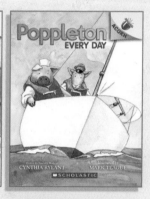

Poppleton
IN SUMMER

Written by Newbery Medalist
CYNTHIA RYLANT

Illustrated by
MARK TEAGUE

ACORN™
SCHOLASTIC INC.

Library of Congress Cataloging-in-Publication Data

Names: Rylant, Cynthia, author. I Teague, Mark, illustrator. I Rylant,
Cynthia. Poppleton ; 6.
Title: Poppleton in summer / written by Newbery Medalist Cynthia Rylant ;
illustrated by Mark Teague.
Description: New York : Acorn/Scholastic, 2023. I Series: Poppleton ; 6 I
Summary: Poppleton the pig enjoys the summer by relaxing on his rooftop, taking a drive
with his friend Hudson, and enjoying summer rain.
Identifiers: LCCN 2018055826 I ISBN 9781338566758 (pb) I ISBN 9781338566765 (hc)
Subjects: LCSH: Poppleton (Fictitious character)—Juvenile fiction. I
Swine—Juvenile fiction. I Summer—Juvenile fiction. I
Friendship—Juvenile fiction. I CYAC: Pigs—Fiction. I Summer—Fiction. I
Friendship—Fiction.
Classification: LCC PZ7.R982 Pwm 2020 I DDC 813.54 [E] —dc23
LC record available at https://lccn.loc.gov/2018055826

10 9 8 7 6 5 4 3 2 1   23 24 25 26 27

Printed in China   62
First printing, May 2023
Edited by Katie Carella and Megan Peace
Book design by Maria Mercado

CONTENTS

MEET THE CHARACTERS

Poppleton

Cherry Sue

Hudson

PINK

It was summer.

Poppleton loved lying on his roof in summer.

It was his favorite way to relax.

But one day he fell asleep and stayed
on the roof a bit too long.

When he woke up,
his pale pig body was **pink**!

"Why are you so pink, Poppleton?"
asked his neighbor Cherry Sue.

"I fell asleep in the sun, and now
I look like a rose," said Poppleton.

"You do not look like a rose,"
said Cherry Sue.

"Thank goodness," said Poppleton.

"But maybe a strawberry,"
said Cherry Sue.

"What?" said Poppleton.

"Just kidding," said Cherry Sue.
"Besides, you still have a nice smile."

Poppleton smiled.

"And you still have kind eyes," said Cherry Sue.

Poppleton blinked.

"And don't forget," said Cherry Sue, "you're a smashing dresser."

"I am?" asked Poppleton.

Cherry Sue was the best friend.

Poppleton got an idea.

"Wait here," he said.

Poppleton went inside.

He put on his best suit.

He put on his best hat.

He looked kindly in the mirror
and smiled his best smile.

Even a slightly pink pig can take
a good friend out to lunch.
And he did!

THE JEEP

Poppleton wanted to go to the country.

He wanted to hear a cow moo.

He wanted to smell some hay.

13

"Would you like to go to the country for the day?" he asked his friend Hudson.

"Sure!" said Hudson.
"How will we get there?"

"I'll rent a jeep," said Poppleton.

15

Poppleton rented a jeep.
It sat very high.

"I feel so tall!" said Hudson.

Off they went.

Poppleton felt like a different pig in a jeep.

He felt strong.

He felt brave.

He stopped at a store to get sunglasses.

Now he felt even stronger and even braver.

He decided to impress Hudson.

"See that hill over there?"
Poppleton said.
"I am going to drive over it."

Poppleton drove the jeep off the road and over the hill.

"Wow!" said Hudson.

"See that stream over there?"
Poppleton said.
"I am going to drive through it."

Poppleton drove the jeep
through the stream.

"Wow!" said Hudson.

"See that field over there?"
Poppleton said.
"I am going to drive across it."

But Hudson said,
"I don't know, Poppleton.
It sure looks muddy."

"I can handle it," said Poppleton.

"We might get stuck," said Hudson.

"I can handle it," said Poppleton.

He drove across the field . . .

. . . and got stuck.

Some cows came by to laugh.

"We get a stuck jeep here every week!"
they said. "And it's always somebody
wearing sunglasses!"

Hudson looked at Poppleton.

"Can you push?" he asked.

"I can handle it," said Poppleton glumly.

Poppleton tried to push the jeep out of the mud.

He lost his sunglasses, and his clothes got muddy.

"We will help!" said the cows.

The cows did a good job un-sticking the jeep.

So Poppleton and Hudson shared their double-decker picnic sandwiches with them.

Then the two friends had a
nice, quiet drive back home.

THE RAIN

Poppleton loved a summer shower.

He loved to sit on his front porch and watch.

The rain went **picka picka picka**
on the roof.

Poppleton always caught some
of the summer rain in a little bucket.
He saved it for his indoor plants.

41

"Some summer rain for you,"
he told his green ivy.

The ivy grew greener.

"Some summer rain for you,"
he told his violet.

The violet turned bright purple.

"Some summer rain for you,"
he told his morning glory.

The morning glory flowers opened wide.

Poppleton thought.
"I wonder what would happen
if **I** drank summer rain?"

He took a little drink.

Then he looked in the mirror.

Did his eyes grow browner?

Maybe.

He looked more closely.

Did his nose turn pinker?

Maybe.

Then he opened wide.

His teeth were dazzling!

Maybe summer rain did work for pigs!

So Poppleton took

his browner eyes

and pinker nose

and dazzling teeth

for a happy summer walk.

ABOUT THE CREATORS

CYNTHIA RYLANT

has written more than one hundred books, including *Dog Heaven*, *Cat Heaven*, and the Newbery Medal–winning novel *Missing May*. She lives with her pets in Oregon.

MARK TEAGUE

lives in New York State with his family, which includes a dog and two cats, but no pigs, llamas, or goats, and only an occasional mouse. Mark is the author of many books and the illustrator of many more, including the How Do Dinosaurs series.

YOU CAN DRAW

1. Draw an egg shape with the wide end at the bottom. Use a pencil and draw lightly! (You will need to erase most of this as you go.)

2. Add these rough shapes for arms and feet and a shirt. (Can you tell that Hudson is waving at you?)

3. Make a head shape — another egg, but with the wide end up this time.

4. Add ears and a nose — remember, draw lightly so you can erase!

HUDSON!

5. Draw the eyes — and a smile! Add a shirt.

6. Add fingers and toes. Finish the ears.

7. Finish the shirt. Add a tail. Finish the picture by adding shadows and whiskers.

8. Color in your drawing!

WHAT'S YOUR STORY?

Poppleton and Hudson take a trip to the country.
Imagine **you** and Poppleton go on a road trip.
What would your car look like?
Where would you go?
Write and draw your story!